characters created by

lauren child

WhoOps! But it wasn't Me

PUFFIN

Text based on script written by

Bridget Hurst and Carol Noble

Illustrations from the TV animation

produced by Tiger Aspect

PUFFIN BOOKS
Published by the Penguin Group: London, New York, Australia,
Canada, India, Ireland, New Zealand and South Africa
Penguin Books Ltd, Registered Offices: 80 Strand, London WC2R 0RL, England

puffinbooks.com

First published 2006
Published in this edition 2008
3 5 7 9 10 8 6 4 2
Text and illustrations copyright © Lauren Child/Tiger Aspect Productions Limited, 2006
The Charlie and Lola logo is a trademark of Lauren Child
All rights reserved
The moral right of the author/illustrator has been asserted
Made and printed in China
ISBN: 978–1–856–13183–4

This edition produced for The Book People Ltd,
Hall Wood Avenue, Haydock, St Helens WA11 9UL

I have this little sister Lola.
She is small and very funny.
Sometimes Lola likes to play
with my things.
Usually I don't mind.

One day I come home from school
with the best thing I have ever made.

Lola says, "OoooOh!"

I say,
"It took me ten days,
    three hours and forty minutes
to make the outside,
        which is called
the superstructure...

"... It's built from

three **cereal** **packets,**

ten yoghurt pots,

28 bottle tops,

157

sweet wrappers

and a roll of extra-wide tinfoil."

Lola says, "Ooooh!"

I say, "Don't touch it!
This rocket is really breakable.
I don't mind you playing with
most of my things,
but you must double,
triple promise
you'll NEVER play
with it."

"Let's play something
            else then," says Lola.
        I say, "I've promised to play football
            with Marv."
"But what am I going to do?" says Lola.
            And I say, "Why don't you play
        with Soren Lorensen?"

Soren Lorensen is Lola's imaginary friend.
No one can see him except for Lola.

And Lola says,
        "Soren Lorensen always wants
to play with me."

Soren Lorensen says, "Ellie is really **sad** because he doesn't like the nasty **hyenas** laughing at him."

"Those hyenas are meanies, aren't they?" says Lola.
"What are we going to do?"

Soren Lorensen says,
    "Remember to be extra
specially careful, Lola."

And Lola says,

"I am!
I am!"

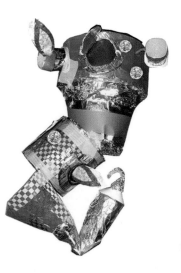

Then she says,

"Oh no!"

Lola looks at the pieces of broken rocket.
"You know, I think that when
things are broken they can always be
mended and made like new..."

"If we both act normally, Lola,
then Charlie might not think
we did it," says Soren Lorensen.

Lola whispers,

"No, he'll never know."

Lola says, "Do you think we should tell him
what really happened?"
Soren Lorensen says, "Maybe we could tell Charlie
somebody else broke the rocket?"
And Lola says, "Yes! Because it is nearly true!"

So Lola comes to talk to me.
"Charlie, Soren Lorensen and me have got something
very **extremely** important to tell you."

I say, "What?"

Lola says,
"It is the real **true** story of who **broke**
your special **rocket**.

"... and then we landed and we were so **squished** that...

the
rocket
just fell
to
Pieces.
And that's
what happened."

I say,

"Right.
I'm going to
tell **Mum!**"

"Oh dear, I don't think he **believed** us," says Soren Lorensen.

Lola says,
"I think I have to tell
Charlie the **truth**. But will it
make Charlie **like** me again?"

Soren Lorensen says,
"As long as you say **sorry** too."

And I say,
"Are you **really**, Lola?"

Lola says, "**Sorry**, Charlie."

And she does look really very sorry.

So I say, "That's OK.
At least you've told the **truth**."

Then Lola sees the rocket.

"You **mend**ed it, Charlie!" she says.

And I say,
"Yes, Lola, I've mended it."

"I like it," says Lola.
I say,
"Don't touch it!"